AN M. NIGHT SHYAMALAN FILM

THE LAST AIRBENDER

BATTLE OF THE NORTH

by Brian James
based on the series *Avatar: The Last Airbender*
created by Michael Dante DiMartino and Bryan Konietzko
based on the screenplay written by M. Night Shyamalan
illustrated by Shane L. Johnson

SIMON AND SCHUSTER

D1513058

SIMON AND SCHUSTER

First published in Great Britain in 2010 by Simon & Schuster UK Ltd

1st Floor, 222 Gray's Inn Road, London WC1X 8HB

Originally published in the USA in 2010 by Simon Spotlight,

an imprint of Simon & Schuster Children's Division, New York.

© 2010 Paramount Pictures. All rights reserved.

The Last Airbender and all related titles, logos and characters are trademarks of Viacom International Inc.

All rights reserved including the right of reproduction in whole or in part in any form.

A CIP catalogue record for this book is available from the British Library

ISBN 978-1-84738-834-6

Printed in the United States of America

10 9 8 7 6 5 4 3 2 1

Visit our websites: www.simonandschuster.co.uk and thelastairbendermovie.com

2

PROLOGUE

If you are reading this, you have found something very sacred to our world—all that is known of the Battle of the North, the legendary battle between the Fire Nation and the Northern Water Tribe, and the struggle leading up to it. This scroll contains valuable information concerning the most important figures in the Fire Nation and its mighty military. It also contains the history of the Water Tribe, its heroic leaders and benders, and all that is known about the Avatar and those who are traveling with him. No one will ever question what happened that fateful day at the Northern Water Tribe, for all that is known about the legendary battle and how it was won has been recorded here, from a secret location within the Earth Kingdom, for all citizens and generations to discover.

It is in your best interest to keep this scroll safe. If the Fire Lord ever learns that these secrets have been exposed, whoever possesses this scroll may be in serious danger. As I write this, the Fire Nation war rages on. You have my word that all the information in this scroll was recounted exactly as it was told to me firsthand. It cannot fall into the wrong hands. Otherwise all will be lost.

Who am I, you ask? That is something I will never reveal.

INTRODUCTION

A time long ago, the four nations of the world lived in peace. The Avatar, master of all four elements, kept balance between the Fire Nation, the Earth Kingdom, the Water Tribes, and the Air Nomads. In each nation there were members who had mastered the art of bending their birth elements, but only the Avatar had the ability to manipulate all four. This special skill allowed the Avatar to prevent any one nation from becoming too powerful.

In addition to being the great peacemaker of the world, the Avatar also served as the bridge to the spirit world. Whenever in need, the Avatar could summon the great spirits and seek their wisdom, which went far beyond that of man. For this reason, the people of the world counted on the Avatar to protect them from injustice. And for many, many lifetimes, that is exactly what the Avatar did.

During this time of peace, the four nations flourished.

In the Earth Kingdom, powerful earthbenders used their ability to build towering cities made of stone. The capital of Ba Sing Se was the most impressive and largest city in the kingdom.

The Water Tribe constructed cities of ice at both

the North and South Poles. Over time, the inhabitants of each frozen region developed their own unique customs and became known as the Northern Water Tribe and the Southern Water Tribe.

The Air Nomads were a society of monks that built temples at the highest locations in the four corners of the world. With their ability to manipulate wind currents, airbenders could easily reach the temples, while Air Nomads without the gift for bending relied on the help of their loyal flying sky bison.

Located on a group of volcanic islands, the Fire Nation remained the most mysterious of the four nations for centuries. Drawing their power from the sun, firebenders mastered the most dangerous of elements. Over time, the Fire Nation learned to use their bending technique to mold and build strong structures. In secret, the Fire Nation began to use this new material to make ships and weapons that were more powerful than any the world had seen before.

Despite the Fire Nation's military advantage, the Avatar was still able to keep the natural balance in order. But that all changed one day when a comet zoomed across the sky and gave firebenders

a moment of great power. The Fire Lord used this opportunity to attack the other nations. Only the Avatar could stop the ruthless firebenders, but when the world needed him most . . . he vanished.

A hundred years have passed since that fateful day, and a year has passed since the Battle of the North was fought. The same comet is set to return in two short years, providing another opportunity for attack. The Fire Nation is nearing victory in the war. But now there is hope . . . for the Avatar has finally returned!

OUR ENEMY: THE FIRE NATION

This wasn't always the case, but for the past one hundred years, the Fire Nation has been the enemy of the rest of the world. Their power has grown immensely, and continues to strengthen every day. The only way to defeat this great enemy is to learn all that there is to know about them. This is all the information I have gathered thus far on the dangerous Fire Nation. . . .

THE FIRE NATION

The Fire Nation remained a mysterious place for many centuries. Among its closely guarded secrets was the ability to mold metal into ships, swords, and other tools. This skill was unknown to the rest of the world—until the Fire Nation unleashed its military might upon the other three nations.

Determined to rule over the other three kingdoms, the Fire Nation army attacked, and quickly gained the upper hand in the war by using its superior metal warships. The rest of the world soon learned of the Fire Nation's ruthless and aggressive nature. The powerful firebenders made their horrifying intentions clear from their first blow. Knowing that the next Avatar would be born into the Air Nomads, the Fire Nation attacked the peaceful Air Temples first. The Fire Lord believed that if the Avatar could be eliminated, there would be no serious obstacle to his plans.

The Fire Nation mercilessly wiped the Air Nomads' noble race from the face of world! But despite the Fire Nation's easy victory, the Avatar was never found. Some people questioned whether the Avatar's spirit had ever been reborn into the Air Nomads, but the Fire Lord remained convinced of the Avatar's existence. Now, one hundred years into the war, the leaders of the Fire Nation continue to search for the missing Avatar.

THE ART OF FIREBENDING

Drawing their power from all heat sources, most notably the sun, firebenders are formidable fighters. Unlike the other forms of bending, firebending is extremely aggressive and lacks nearly any defensive moves. Firebenders attempt to overwhelm their opponents with a barrage of flame and fury. Their punches yield fireballs, and sweeping kicks send long arches of flame shooting toward an opponent.

The source of a firebender's strength is his or her chi—the life force believed to be present in all living things. But, as with the other forms of bending, the ability to bend fire also relies on the nearness of the element. In battle, firebending soldiers stay close to carts filled with burning embers.

On extraordinary occasions, skilled firebenders have been known to create fire from their own chi. This is a highly unusual occurrence. However, there is one time when all firebenders gain this ability—when the comet returns, they are all given a moment of great power.

THE LEADERS OF THE FIRE NATION
Bent on conquering the world, the Fire Nation leaders reject the old belief that all four elements are equal. They also refuse to accept the ancient tradition that humankind should bow to the spirits.

The human world and the spirit world are two different worlds, and the only person who can bridge the gap between the two is the Avatar. The Fire Nation leaders thought that eliminating the Avatar would mean they would never have to deal with the spirit world again. However, they fail to understand the power of the spirits and the Avatar. This causes them to make many mistakes as they attempt to take control. The Fire Nation leaders believe that only a total and complete victory in the war will prove their convictions to the rest of the world.

FIRE LORD OZAI

As the brutal leader of the Fire Nation, Fire Lord Ozai rules his kingdom through fear. He is rarely seen outside the walls of his massive stone palace, but those who do set eyes upon him will likely cower under his menacing gaze. An extremely skilled bender, Fire Lord Ozai is a match against any foe— even the Avatar.

As a military leader, Fire Lord Ozai is merciless. He is willing to sacrifice any number of his own men in order to achieve victory. He believes in discipline and obedience at all costs.

"We no longer need to cower before the spirits like some primitive people."

In addition to being cruel, Fire Lord Ozai is equally arrogant. A firm believer that fire is the strongest of the four elements, he is convinced the spirits have unjustly prevented the Fire Nation from taking its rightful place as the world's ruling power. In a bold move, he ordered a raid on the Great Library, during which the Fire Nation stole scrolls containing secrets of the spirit world. The Fire Lord and his top commander, Zhao, planned to use information from the scrolls to eliminate their enemies and end the spirit world's influence over the living.

COMMANDER ZHAO

Commander Zhao was a fierce-looking man in charge of the Fire Nation army. He shared Fire Lord Ozai's vision and became his most trusted advisor. Zhao propelled the Fire Lord closer to his goal of destroying the spirit world's influence over humankind when he discovered the Great Library—a place long rumored to be only a myth.

"The Fire Lord and I have a plan to ensure our reign and the downfall of our enemies."

Zhao stole many valuable scrolls from the Great Library. These scrolls contain secrets about the spirit world that no one was ever supposed to learn. Zhao planned to use this information to limit the waterbenders' power during the Fire Nation's invasion of the Northern Water Tribe.

PRINCE ZUKO

The firstborn and only son of Fire Lord Ozai, Prince Zuko is the would-be heir to the Fire Nation throne. But Prince Zuko's fate took a drastic turn when he questioned a general's orders in defense of some of his friends who were going to be sacrificed in battle. For his disobedience, he was sentenced to

"One day my father will take me back and you will bow before me."

an Agni-Ki duel where he was supposed to fight the general he'd defied. But when Zuko showed up, he was surprised to discover his father opposite him. When Zuko refused to fight, Fire Lord Ozai banished his son and marked him with a burn scar on the left side of his face to teach Zuko a lesson.

Fire Lord Ozai will not allow Prince Zuko to return to the throne unless he finds the Avatar. Determined to regain his honor, Prince Zuko roams the world in search of the unknown airbender. Many believe his hunt is an impossible task, but Zuko is unrelenting in his quest, willing to do whatever it takes to capture the Avatar—even if it means going up against Fire Nation soldiers.

In order to remain unidentified during conflicts with members of his own nation, Prince Zuko often disguises himself as the mysterious Blue Spirit. Wearing a blue devil mask and wielding two silver swords, the Blue Spirit has long remained a mystery to Fire Nation soldiers.

GENERAL IROH

Once a gifted and respected general in the Fire Nation army, Iroh commanded the Hundred Day Siege of Ba Sing Se. The siege was supposed to be the Fire Nation's greatest victory, but it ended in failure. Iroh returned home in disgrace.

During that battle, Iroh also lost his son. He has since grown close to his nephew, Zuko. When Zuko was banished, Iroh joined the young prince on his quest to find the Avatar. He is convinced that Zuko's destiny is closely tied to that of the Avatar's, and is willing to aid him in whatever way he can.

"To meet a spirit would be a great honor."

Unlike his brother, the Fire Lord, Iroh strongly believes in the old traditions and holds the spirits in great esteem. Iroh thinks there are certain things humankind should not tamper with. The spirits and the spirit world are among them.

Iroh is one of the most powerful benders in the Fire Nation. It is said that he has the ability to create fire using only the force of his chi—even in times when the comet is nowhere to be seen.

THE FIRE NATION MILITARY

The Fire Nation army is well-trained and disciplined. It is armed with weapons created by the many skilled metalworkers in the kingdom. In battle, these weapons can be stronger than bending, leading the Fire Lord to believe that humans have grown stronger than the spirits.

BATTLE STRATEGY

The strategy of the Fire Nation is one of slow build. The destruction of most of the major villages in the Southern Water Tribe followed the conquest of the Air Nomads. An assault on the Earth Kingdom began shortly after that, with the first attacks on small towns and villages, allowing the fear to grow from within. Many villages throughout the Earth Kingdom have fallen under Fire Nation control.

Once in command of the smaller towns and villages, the Fire Nation began outlawing all other forms of bending in other nations. The punishment for defying the law is imprisonment, and the Fire Nation has already imprisoned many benders across the Earth Kingdom.

Meanwhile, they continued to perfect their huge

metal machines and drills back home. Once the smaller towns and villages were taken and their machines were finished, they began to infiltrate the larger cities. One day the Fire Nation hopes to finally take the Earth Kingdom city of Ba Sing Se and the fortress of the Northern Water Tribe.

The day Commander Zhao found the Great Library, he gained some very valuable information from which a new strategy was born. After discovering that the Sun and Moon Spirits took the forms of two koi fish in a sacred pond in the city of the Northern Water Tribe, he and the Fire Lord

decided to kill the Moon Spirit, which would render the waterbenders powerless.

STRENGTHS

Fear has been the Fire Nation's greatest ally in this war. The Fire Nation is also organized, ruthless, and led by one man who gives them focus, unlike the other nations, which fight in small, disorganized groups—or not at all. Firebenders are strongest in the daytime because they get their power from the sun. When the comet arrived one hundred years ago, the Fire Nation was given a moment of great power— enough power to wipe out an entire nation of Air Nomads. It is feared that when the comet returns in two years they will once again be able to create fire and destroy what is left of the remaining nations.

WEAKNESSES

The Fire Lord, and subsequently the rest of the Fire Nation, is driven by the belief that fire is naturally stronger than the other elements. The Fire Lord's inability to understand that all elements are powerful in their own way, and that no one element is more powerful than another, is a great weakness. Exploiting this weakness will be our path to victory. Another weakness is that firebending is less powerful at night and in wet weather conditions. Fighting in the battle at the Northern Water Tribe played on this weakness, as the snow and ice helped to diffuse some of the fire.

SOLDIERS

The Fire Nation army is made up of thousands of soldiers. There are a variety of different types: simple guards, skilled archers, and firebenders. Guards are armed and form the first line of defense that any attacker must get through. These

guards also man the prison yards in which benders from other nations are held captive. No matter where a battle takes place, it is certain that skilled archers will stand atop the highest points to shoot at attackers from afar. Finally, skilled firebenders are prepared to stop at nothing to take down an attacker. No matter to which category a soldier belongs, they all share a dedication to discipline and an unwavering loyalty to the Fire Lord.

WARSHIPS

The Fire Nation armada is perhaps its greatest source of strength. These massive ships are built with metal hulls that allow them to break through the ocean's icy waters. Powered by fire, these ships are much faster than the boats used by the Water Tribe and are nearly impossible to defeat. They are also equipped with telescopes, so the Fire Nation can spy from afar.

KOMODO-RHINO

These large beasts are half rhino and half Komodo lizards. Native to the Fire Nation, these animals are used by the military for transportation. Like the soldiers, the Komodo-rhinos wear metal armor for protection.

WEAPONS

The development of metalworking has allowed the Fire Nation to create an array of useful weapons. Soldiers without bending abilities are no longer helpless, as they were in generations past. Armed with swords, spears, and other blades, these soldiers have the ability to strike fear into the hearts of their enemies. Fire Nation swords can be as large as thirty inches long, expertly made from strong, sharp metal. Other advancements have led to the creation of metal drills that allow ships and soldiers to burrow through earth and ice to reach the once impenetrable fortresses in the Earth Kingdom and Northern Water Tribe.

OUR ALLIES:
THE AVATAR AND
THE WATER TRIBE

Though the Fire Nation has destroyed the Air Nomads and taken over many small towns and villages in the Earth Kingdom and Southern Water Tribe, up until now they have yet to conquer any of the other nations' major cities. The Northern Water Tribe stands strong and is surrounded by an ice fortress. As the Avatar and his friends traveled north, the world looked to the Water Tribe to defend its icy fortress from the Fire Nation. This is what I know of our defenders. . . .

THE AVATAR

The Avatar is the only one who can keep the peace among all four nations. He or she is also the only one who can bend all four elements. Only the Avatar can go back and forth between the spirit world and the human world. When an Avatar dies, his or her spirit is reborn. To make sure the balance between the elements remains, the new Avatar is born into the next element in the cycle. The Avatar before Aang was named Roku. He was a firebender. Before him, the Avatar was Kyoshi. She was an earthbender. They were both legendary masters of all the elements.

AVATAR AANG

"I ran away. I'm sorry. But I'm back now."

Aang is thirteen years old, and he is the new Avatar. He is also the last of the Air Nomads. The monks of the Southern Air Temple raised him. Monk Gyatso was known to be his closest teacher. He

was like a father to Aang. He taught him all about airbending. When Aang was eight, he learned to use air currents for balance. He also learned to meditate for long periods of time. That's how he earned his airbending tattoos.

When they suspected he might be the Avatar, the monks gave Aang a test. They put a thousand toys in front of him and asked him to choose four. Even though there were so many to pick from, Aang chose the same four toys that the previous Avatars had played with when they were children. It was then that the monks knew they were right.

Unlike most Avatars before him, Aang wasn't prepared to accept his responsibilities as the Avatar right away. He learned that as the Avatar, he could never have a family or fall in love. His responsibilities would be too great, and he would always be expected to sacrifice himself for the greater good. It was too much for him to take.

So he decided to run away. It is rumored that he didn't intend to stay away, however, nature intervened and he became trapped in the icy waters of the South Pole. He froze, and remained frozen there for a hundred years.

Once he was found, Aang discovered the danger that the world is in. It is believed that he has changed, and that he has finally accepted his responsibilities as the Avatar—that he intends to fight the Fire Nation and save our world. However, at the time that Aang ran away he could only bend air. He learned waterbending in time for the battle at the Northern Water Tribe, and has to learn how to bend the other two elements before the comet returns in two years and the Fire Nation becomes more powerful than ever before.

APPA

Appa is the last known flying sky bison, and he is loyal to Aang. Back in a time when the Air Normads flourished, these animals were a common sight in the skies. In addition to being a fast way to travel, flying sky bison are very faithful companions. The Air Nomads summon them with whistles that can only be heard by the animals. They are always near their companion humans, ready to help them whenever they are in danger.

THE ART OF AIRBENDING

Airbending is the most defensive of the four forms of bending. Airbenders are a peaceful group and primarily use their bending skills for self defense. However, that doesn't mean airbending is any less powerful than bending the other elements.

Airbenders learn to feel the energy behind the wind, not just the breeze on their skin. An airbender

plants his feet, pulls at the air—like pulling at an imaginary rope—and is able to send air rushing forward. By whipping his hands from right to left, an airbender can control the direction of this wind, easily deflecting fire or water in a fight. The wind currents can also be used to avoid an attack from an earthbender.

Before Aang returned, airbending was thought to be a lost art. As a result, Aang is known as the Last Airbender. None of Aang's enemies are familiar with this style of bending. This is an advantage Aang has been able to use in his quest to defeat the Fire Lord.

Aang also uses his Air Nomad staff, a special tool developed by the Air Nomads, to help him glide through the air. It looks like a normal wooden staff at first sight, but by tapping it just right, wings emerge from the sides of the staff and it quickly transforms into a small glider. Airbenders manipulate the wind currents and use their gliders to travel great distances through the air.

THE WATER TRIBE

In the distant past, the Water Tribe existed as one nation located at the North Pole. Many centuries ago, a small number of people left the North Pole and set up a colony on the other side of the world at the South Pole. Over time, the two peoples developed different customs and ways of life. As a result, the Water Tribe split in two, into the Northern Water Tribe and the Southern Water Tribe.

The Northern Water Tribe was led by Princess Yue. She took over after her father died. With the help of the tribe's skilled waterbenders, Princess Yue managed to keep the Northern Water Tribe safe from the ravages of the ongoing war for many years. Up until recently, the mighty Fire Nation hadn't dared to attack the Northern Water Tribe's fortified city.

Their stronghold is constructed entirely of ice that was shaped by benders and is protected from an ocean invasion by a huge ice wall.

Unlike their sister tribe to the north, the Southern Water Tribe has been decimated by the war. The people of the Southern Water Tribe did not live in fortified cities. Most of them lived in small villages of igloos nestled in ice valleys. The Fire Nation easily overran these villages in the early days of the war and removed all waterbenders.

THE ART OF WATERBENDING

Waterbenders get their strength from the Moon Spirit and the Ocean Spirit, and grow stronger once the moon has risen. Just as these two spirits live together in balance, waterbending is a balanced art form—equally as defensive as it is offensive.

The ability to manipulate water yields some spectacular moves. Whipping the hands back and then thrusting them forward will produce a tight stream of water. A waterbender uses this stream to attack and defend. A strong punching motion will produce water cannonball blasts. Benders can also freeze the water under their control. This skill allows waterbenders to create shields and ice prisons, and even gives them the ability to surf along ice streams and streak across the battlefield in a flash.

Waterbenders draw on their emotions to gain more power. By letting their emotions flow like the water, benders are able to better master their art. When traveling over land, waterbenders carry small pouches around their waists filled with water so that they are never without their element.

THE LEADERS OF THE WATER TRIBE

Peaceful in nature, the Water Tribe would have preferred to stay out of the Fire Nation's war altogether. However, raids on the Southern Water Tribe motivated its warriors into action. The Northern Water Tribe managed to stay removed

from battle for almost one hundred years, but finally, one fateful day, the Fire Nation attacked—like we all knew it would!

KATARA

Though only fifteen years old, Katara is an extremely important member of the Southern Water Tribe. In fact, she's the last waterbender left in the tribe. Without a master bender to teach her, Katara traveled to the North Pole along with the Avatar.

There she studied with Master Pakku and learned the art of waterbending in order to help her people.

Katara doesn't like to fight, but she won't back down from one either—especially one with the Fire Nation! She can't stand the way the Fire Nation bullies

"Sokka and I can be your family, Aang."

the other nations. Her own mother was taken away in a Fire Nation raid on their village many years ago. She wears a necklace her mother gave her. It is engraved with an ancient Water Tribe symbol, and it is her dearest possession. It's the only reminder she has left of her mother, and Katara is convinced this emotional connection improves her bending.

Unlike most, Katara always believed that one day the Avatar would return and put an end to the Fire Nation's cruelty. But even Katara had no idea how closely her fate would be tied to Aang's.

Along with her brother, Sokka, Katara has joined the Avatar on his quest to master all four elements. The three have become very close, forming a kind of makeshift family as they travel the world. But Aang's feelings for Katara have grown very strong during their time together. One day he'll have to make a choice between being with Katara and being the Avatar.

SOKKA

Sokka is a born leader who is always up for a battle. When his father left the Southern Water Tribe to join the Earth Kingdom's fight against the Fire Nation, Sokka was given the task of protecting their small village. Though he's not a bender, Sokka is a fearless fighter. He wields a boomerang, specially made by Southern Water Tribe craftsmen, as his weapon of choice. With the help of his sister, Katara, Sokka succeeded in keeping their village safe—until the two of them accidentally discovered the Avatar frozen inside a floating block of sea ice.

The Avatar's presence in their little

"We started a rebellion."

village quickly drew the attention of the Fire Nation. After their firsthand encounter with the ruthless Fire Nation, the siblings decided to join the fight. While traveling with the Avatar, Sokka proved his leadership by inspiring the people of the Earth Kingdom to resist the Fire Nation. "That's how you win a war—by fighting on the big fronts and from the inside," he told them.

Sokka has suffered his share of loss during the war. Rather than discouraging him, these sacrifices have made Sokka more determined than ever to put an end to the Fire Nation's plans to conquer the world.

PRINCESS YUE

Princess Yue was the ruler of the Northern Water Tribe and played a key role in the legendary battle there. She took over leading the tribe when her father died, and was very effective in keeping her people free from Fire Nation aggression.

She could be easily identified by her pure white hair. Legend has it that when Princess Yue was born, she did not move or make a sound. Her mother and father prayed to the Moon Spirit for days before dipping her into the sacred waters of the spirit's pond. It is said that her hair turned white as the spirit poured life into her. As a result, her destiny was forever linked with the Moon Spirit.

"There is no love without sacrifice."

When Commander Zhao harmed the Moon Spirit during the Fire Nation's attack, Princess Yue faced a tough decision. Without the Moon Spirit, the balance of power in the world was in danger. At such a young age, the burden of figuring out how to save the Moon Spirit fell on her shoulders, a weight she carried with great dignity.

MASTER PAKKU

Master Pakku is known to be the greatest

waterbender in the entire Northern Water Tribe. In battle, he uses water like two whips, snapping them like tentacles at his opponent. His superior skills allow Master Pakku to take on many enemies at once.

Master Pakku trains all the most promising waterbenders in the Northern Water Tribe. He stresses to his students that they must dig deep inside themselves and allow their emotions to run through them if they ever hope to master the art of waterbending. When Katara and Aang came to the

"To master water, you must release your emotions."

North Pole, he took on the task of training them as well. It is considered a great honor for a master to teach the Avatar. Under Pakku's training, Aang was quickly able to master the art of bending water, the second in his quest to learn to bend all four elements.

THE WATER TRIBE AND ALLIED FORCES

The men of the Southern Water Tribe left home to join the warfront after most of the Southern Water Tribe was destroyed by the Fire Nation. They sailed away on small ships with whatever weapons they could make. Their lack of bending abilities puts them at a disadvantage against benders.

In addition to the Southern Water Tribe men, various small groups of fighters have tried to defeat the Fire Nation to no avail. A group of Earth Kingdom warriors, who call themselves the Kyoshi warriors, have been a small but valiant force in some Earth Kingdom villages. These brave warriors helped the Avatar and his friends make it safely through the Earth Kingdom on their way to the Northern Water Tribe.

BATTLE STRATEGY

Unfortunately, the battle strategy of our allies and fighters is much less organized than that of our enemy. However, since the Avatar's return, a strategy of hope has been slowly spreading through the nations. The Avatar has begun revealing himself to those who he meets along his journey, in an effort to renew people's hope and resolve to fight back. If people know about the Avatar's return, they will be more likely to believe that the Fire Nation can be defeated. This belief will help to strike down the fear that the Fire Nation continues to instill in all citizens of other nations.

STRENGTHS

Unlike the Fire Lord, our allies understand the importance of all elements in the cycle, and believe in the power of the Avatar. Water is a particularly powerful element to oppose fire, as it has the power to extinguish flames. (In the battle of the Northern Water Tribe, waterbenders had an advantage because the battle took place on their grounds, where they were surrounded by water and ice.)

WEAKNESSES

Waterbenders of the Northern Water Tribe are significantly outnumbered by the Fire Nation army. The Fire Lord's blatant disregard for the spirit world and the Avatar means that he will continue to employ strategies to win this war that other nations wouldn't dream of using.

TRANSPORTATION

The Water Tribe ships are much less advanced than those of the Fire Nation. Fighters mainly travel by

small, wooden canoes, however, both the Southern and Northern Water Tribes have some medium-size ships as well. But they have nothing to compare to the strength and durability of the Fire Nation's metal warships.

WEAPONS

Wooden spears with tips of bone or stone, blades, and knives make up the Water Tribe's primary weapons. Sokka has also been known to use his boomerang for offensive maneuvers during battle. Usually carved from animal bones or teeth, boomerangs like Sokka's are specially made and ornately carved by members of the Southern Water Tribe.

THE BATTLE
OF THE NORTH

The legend of the battle comes to me in bits and pieces, from various fighters, enemies, and defenders alike. This is all I know of the circumstances of the infamous Battle of the North. . . .

THE FORTRESS

The Northern Water Tribe is surrounded by a fortress of ice. To one side of this fortress stand snow-capped mountains, to the other, a vast body of water. The fortress was built by the waterbenders of

the Northern Water Tribe. It spans several miles in width, and is at least two stories high. It is protected by walls and gates made of ice, which can only be controlled by waterbending guards. Throughout the fortress, waterbenders built a series of canals through which their boats can travel in and out of the city. If any of the protective measures are broken, someone will sound an alarm to alert the citizens to approaching danger.

THE BATTLE

The Avatar and his friends had been safe in the Northern Water Tribe for some time; the Avatar was learning waterbending with Master Pakku. One day, a warning bell sounded throughout the entire Northern Water Tribe fortress. An intruder was present. The Northern Water Tribe soldiers rushed to the top of the wall, where they were greeted by an armada of Fire Nation ships below. The soldiers quickly rushed to ready the rest of the army.

Little did the Fire Nation know, when the armada arrived at the great ice wall protecting the Water Tribe, Prince Zuko was secretly aboard one of the ships, determined to capture the Avatar before Commander Zhao. So before the assault began, Prince Zuko dove into the icy waters alone and made his way into the city undetected.

Meanwhile, the Avatar searched for a spiritual place to meditate so he could enter the spirit world. He was overheard telling Princess Yue that he needed to speak to a dragon spirit. Princess Yue took him at once to the most spiritual place she could think of. It was a courtyard filled with green grass and luscious trees, surrounded by ice walls twenty

feet high; its warm temperature was left untouched by the frozen winds of the North. At the center of the courtyard was a small koi pond. In it, two koi fish—one white with a black spot, one black with a white spot—swam in circles around each other.

As the Avatar drifted off into the spirit world, Prince Zuko tracked him down in the sacred courtyard, only to be greeted unkindly by the Avatar's good friend, Katara. But Zuko was determined. He set the grass on fire with the torch he was carrying, and then sent a burst of flame directly toward Katara. Using water from the pond, she sent a stream of water into the air to meet Zuko's fire. The two elements met in midair, where they turned into steam.

Then Zuko whipped both arms out to his sides and sent two blasts of fire into the air, each curving toward Katara from opposite directions. She was able to extinguish the first burst of flame, but not the second. It struck her and knocked her violently to the ground. Zuko lunged for the Avatar, grabbing him swiftly even though Aang was still in his meditative state. Zuko carried him to a small storage room just north of the city where he waited, watching the fire bursts coming from the city below. Zuko didn't have to wait for long. The Avatar soon awoke, but before Zuko could fire at him, the Avatar was up and flying. Zuko threw flame after flame, but he never hit anywhere near the boy. Suddenly, water burst out from inside of barrels located in the storage room and rose up and surrounded Zuko. In an instant, the water turned to ice and he was trapped. Katara had found Zuko's hiding place and defeated him, and there was nothing he could do but watch helplessly as she escaped with the Avatar.

On land, the Fire Nation warships sent barrage after barrage of flaming cannonballs into the city, forcing the waterbenders to abandon the giant ice wall separating their city from the ocean. This gave the Fire Nation soldiers an opening. The black-clad firebender soldiers dove into the water armed with metal drills. They broke through the ice behind enemy lines, and soon the fighters of the Northern Water Tribe were overwhelmed.

As the sun began to set and the moon began to rise, the tide slowly shifted. The waterbenders began growing stronger. However, Commander Zhao had no fear. He was on his way to the very same sacred courtyard where the Avatar had meditated—only Zhao was on his way to kill the Moon Spirit. He intended to use the information he had stolen from the Great Library to locate the Moon Spirit koi fish and kill it, weakening the waterbenders enough for the Fire Nation to overcome them. And so Commander Zhao found the Moon and Ocean Spirits and carried out the Fire Lord's evil plan. He killed the Moon Spirit koi fish, causing the moon to turn bright red.

A Fire Nation victory looked close at hand. The waterbenders had lost their power and the fight was nearly over—until Uncle Iroh interfered. Iroh, one of the only Fire Nation leaders to understand the power of the spirits and the Avatar cycle, believed the Fire Lord had gone too far. In a fit of extreme rage, he fought off Commander Zhao and drove him away from the sacred courtyard. Legend has it

that the great Iroh produced fire from his own chi, pounding Zhao with flames that shot straight out of the palms of his hands. Iroh then knew he had to restore the balance of the four powers. To do so, the Moon Spirit needed to be brought back to life. Iroh explained to Princess Yue and her friends that since Yue had been given life as a young child by the Moon Spirit, some of the spirit still lived inside her. So she decided to give her life back to the Moon Spirit in order to save her tribe—and the world—from the Fire Nation. Once Princess Yue offered herself to the moon, the little Moon Spirit koi fish began to move again, the moon returned to its rightful color, and balance was restored to the universe.

With the waterbenders' power restored and the Avatar joining the fight, the advantage quickly shifted back to the side of the Water Tribe. In an amazing feat of mastery, the Avatar moved his hands in high arcs again and again until the entire ocean began to rise under his control. The water rose like a wall, towering into the sky. Then the Avatar changed his movements and the water began to curl, forming a tidal wave. A shadow fell over the entire Fire Nation fleet, and the ships had to reverse course to avoid being washed away. The Avatar had truly mastered water and the world was safe—for now—from complete domination of the Fire Nation.

It was reported that Commander Zhao did not survive the attempted invasion, but that Uncle Iroh and Prince Zuko must have escaped, for they were nowhere to be found in the aftermath of the battle. Thanks to Princess Yue's selfless sacrifice, the Battle of the North was won by our defenders, though much damage was done.

EPILOGUE

All I know of the battle has been inscribed in the pages of this scroll. As I write, the war continues. The Avatar is still free, continuing on his journey to master all four elements before the comet comes again. The Fire Lord is more furious than ever, still searching for ways to end the Avatar's life and win the war. And legend has it that Prince Zuko and his uncle are still roaming the world, also in search of the Avatar. Keep this scroll safe. Show it to your allies, for they should know, as we do now, that the Avatar has unparalleled powers, and they should know the truth about the Battle of the North. Remember that knowledge is power. In the right hands, knowledge creates hope which leads to victory. In the wrong hands, it means disaster for all.